I am a little bear.

François Crozat

W9-CGO-483

BARRON'S

I am a little bear.

I live with my family in a large forest.

This morning, Mama let me go dow
to the river with my brother.

We are so happy, we run all the way!

Bears often go to the river
to catch fish.

Mmmm. That one looks really good!

I would like to catch a fish, too —
but they swim so fast!

And the rocks near the water
re very slippery.

Ooops! . . . I fall in with a splash!

It's a good thing the water
is not too deep.

We find a patch of tasty raspberries.

My brother likes them, too.

After lunch, we pretend to fight.
We growl at each other ferociously.

Mama Porcupine tells her baby not to worry — our growling is all in fun!

Now we are tired,
so we take a little nap.

How can I get that fly off my brother's nose without waking him up?

Help! A strange animal is coming.

He may want to eat us!

Mama comes over to see what's wron
"What cowards you are," she says.

This tiny mouse can't hurt anyone!"

Just look at these beautiful white
butterflies. I try to catch them.

But why are they so cold?
Can this be snow?

It is time to find a place to sleep during the long, cold winter.